W9-ADV-796

Y 811.54 BRO
Brown, Margaret Wise,
Goodnight songs treasury :a collecti
of bedtime poems /

11/19/19

Goodnight Songs Treasury

A Collection of Bedtime Poems

by Margaret Wise Brown

Illustrated by Twenty-Four Award-Winning Picture Book Artists

STERLING CHILDREN'S BOOKS

New York

STERLING CHILDREN'S BOOKS
New York

An Imprint of Sterling Publishing Co., Inc.
1166 Avenue of the Americas
New York, NY 10036

STERLING CHILDREN'S BOOKS and the distinctive Sterling Children's Books logo are registered trademarks of Sterling Publishing Co., Inc.

Text and lyrics © 2014, 2015 by Hollins University
Illustration for "The Mouse's Prayer" © 2014 Jonathan Bean; Illustration for "When I Close My Eyes at Night" © 2014 Carin Berger; Illustration for "Mambian Melody" © 2014 Sophie Blackall; Illustration for "Goat on the Mountain" © 2014 Linda Bleck; Illustration for "Love Song of the Little Bear" © 2015 Peter Brown; Illustration for cover and "To a Child" © 2015 Floyd Cooper; Illustration for "Fall of the Year" © 2015 Leo Espinosa; Illustration for "The Song of the Tiny Cat" © 2015 Blanca Gómez; Illustration for "Advice to Bunnies" © 2015 Molly Idle; Illustration for the title page and "The Noon Balloon" © 2014 Renate Liwska; Illustration for "Cherry Tree" © 2015 Elly McKay; Illustration for "Wooden Town" © 2014 Christopher Silas Neal; Illustration for "Little Donkey Close Your Eyes" © 2014 Zachariah Ohora; Illustration for "Song of Estyn" © 2014 Eric Puybaret; Illustration for "When the Man in the Moon Was a Little Boy" © 2014 Sean Qualls; Illustration for "Sleep Like a Rabbit" © 2014 Isabel Roxas; Illustration for "Quiet in the Wilderness" © 2015 Dadu Shin; Illustration for "Bunny Jig" © 2015 David Small; Illustration for "The Kitten's Dream" © 2015 Bob Staake; Illustration for "The Secret Song" © 2014 Melissa Sweet; Illustration for "Buzz, Buzz, Buzz" © 2015 Satoe Tone; Illustration for "Snowfall" © 2015 Frank Viva; Illustration for "Winter Adventure: © 2015 Mick Wiggins; Illustration for "Sounds in the Night" © 2014 Dan Yaccarino.

All rights reserved. No part of this publication may be reproduced, stored in a retrieval system, or transmitted in any form or by any means (including electronic, mechanical, photocopying, recording, or otherwise) without prior written permission from the publisher.

ISBN 978-1-4549-3477-6

Distributed in Canada by Sterling Publishing Co., Inc.
c/o Canadian Manda Group, 664 Annette Street
Toronto, Ontario M6S 2C8, Canada
Distributed in the United Kingdom by GMC Distribution Services
Castle Place, 166 High Street, Lewes, East Sussex BN7 1XU, England
Distributed in Australia by NewSouth Books, University of New South Wales
Sydney, NSW 2052, Australia

For information about custom editions, special sales, and premium and corporate purchases, please contact Sterling Special Sales at 800-805-5489 or specialsales@sterlingpublishing.com.

Manufactured in China

Lot #:
2 4 6 8 10 9 7 5 3 1
07/19

sterlingpublishing.com

Design by Julie Robine

introduction

argaret Wise Brown, the bestselling author of Goodnight Moon, The Runaway Bunny, and so many other beloved children's books, is universally recognized as one of the foremost authors of children's literature. She was a prolific writer who dreamed stories at night and hurried to write them down in the morning before she forgot them. When she died unexpectedly at the age of forty-two after a routine appendectomy, she had been writing for only fifteen years but had published nearly 100 books.

Margaret was always drawn to music. Her diaries are filled with lyrics that inspired her, and as a young child she had a fondness for putting poems and stories to music she liked. She once said that if she could sing the words to a poem or story she wrote, she knew it had the right tempo. Near the end of her life, she became focused on writing songs for children. As she listened to children go about their lives, she realized that they made up songs about whatever it was they were doing at the time. She wanted to capture that spirit of a child's world in her songs the way she had in stories. She thought if she could do that, perhaps children could retain that ability to express their thoughts in song, something that seems to disappear as we grow older.

Margaret's success as a children's writer is due, in part, to finding words that ring true to a child's ear, but she especially strove to touch a child's heart. To do that, she said she had to write straight from her own heart—she had to love what a child loved. She said about her writing: "One can but hope to make a child laugh or feel clear and happy-headed as he follows the simple rhythm to its logical end. It can jog him with the unexpected and comfort him with the familiar, lift him for a few minutes from his own problems of shoelaces that won't tie, and busy parents and mysterious clock time, into the world of a bug or a bear or a bee or a boy living in the timeless world of a story."

After her death in 1952, Margaret's musical scores and song lyrics along with hundreds of unpublished poem fragments and manuscripts were packed in a trunk in her sister's barn where they sat for decades. Two dozen of these works are now collected together for the first time in Goodnight Songs Treasury. I am certain that Margaret would be thrilled to see that her words have been brought to life so beautifully through music and illustration.

—Amy Gary

Editor, Margaret Wise Brown papers

to a child

Some fine day, just run away
To a long unscheduled day
To where great clouds go sailing by
Above the birds and butterfly.

High, high, high up in the sky
Through the drift of endless blue
A soft white cloud will carry you
High, high, high in the soft, soft air.

the noon balloon

The Noon Balloon
Will be leaving soon
For the sun or the moon.
And wherever it goes,
It will get there too soon.

Aboard was a bear
And a crazy baboon
In the Noon Balloon.
And a monkey, a troll,
And a tiny little mole
On a trip to the moon.

And to lands far away
From Every Day,
Where they could arrive
But never stay
For long.

So the Noon Balloon
Is returning soon
From the sun or the moon.
And whenever it comes,
It will get here too soon.

And to lands far away
From Every Day,
Where they could arrive
But never stay
For long.

So the Noon Balloon
Is returning soon
From the sun or the moon.
And whenever it comes,
It will get here too soon.

the song of the tiny cat

There was a cat—a magic cat
Who was so small, so small
That he was no bigger than a pussy willow!
He used a ladybug for a pillow
And on moonlit nights
In the early spring
When the peepers peep
You would hear him sing,
On bright moonlit nights
In the soft early spring.

"O pussy willows,"
The kitten would sing,
"Gray pussy willows,
First sign of spring.
You come with the spring
All furry and warm
Then summer begins
And poof, you're gone."

"O pussy willows,"
The kitten would purr,
"Magic flowers
All covered with fur,
Now you are here,
Then you disappear.
You disappear
For another long year."

"O little fur flowers
That grow in the spring,
Your secret is kept
By the wild birds that sing.
Till spring comes again
And you will return.
When spring comes again
Then you will return."

There was a cat—a magic cat
Who was so small, so small
That he was no bigger than a pussy willow!
He used a ladybug for a pillow
And on moonlit nights
In the early spring
When the peepers peep
You would hear him sing,
On bright moonlit nights
In the soft early spring.

Mambian
Melody

Hum me a Mambian melody,
Soft as the song of a sleepy bee
In a cloudy pink apple tree.
Hum me a Mambian melody.

Hum me a Mambian melody,
Clear to the ear of love, so dear,
Clear as stars by which sailors steer
On a windy Mambian mountainous sea.
Hum me a Mambian melody.

Hum me a Mambian melody,
Soft as the song of a sleepy bee
In a cloudy pink apple tree.
Hum me a Mambian melody.

Hum me a Mambian melody,
Clear to the ear of love, so dear,
Clear as stars by which sailors steer
On a windy Mambian mountainous sea.

Hum me a Mambian melody.

Love
Song
of the
Little
Bear

By the clear waters
One morning in May
A little bear was singing
In words that seemed to say,

"It's a long time that I've loved you.
Never, never go away.

"It's a long time that I've loved you
And if I seem to stray
It's only that I'm watching
The flowers bloom in May.

"It's a long time that I've loved you.
Never, never go away.

"The birds are singing sweetly,
The robin and the jay.
It's only you I'm loving
On this bright green day.

"It's a long time that I've loved you.
Never, never go away.

"Float little glass bottles
On waters green and gray.
Float little glass bottles
With messages that say:

It's a long time that I've loved you
Never, never go away."

That is the little love song
Of the little bear today
Whose four fur feet are walking
Through these green fields of May.

"It's a long time that I've loved you.
Never, never go away.

"That is my little love song
And all I have to say.

"It's a long time that I've loved you
Never, never go away."

Goat on the MOUNTAIN

A goat on the mountain, a goat on the hill
Drank his little supper and drank his fill.
And the goat on the mountain and the goat on the hill
Went to sleep and the night was still.
The stars shone down from the mountain and the hill.

A goat on the mountain, a goat on the hill
Drank his little supper and drank his fill.
And the goat on the mountain and the goat on the hill
Went to sleep and the night was still.
The stars shone down from the mountain and the hill.

BUZZ, BUZZ, BUZZ

Buzz, Buzz, Buzz
Dream in the solemn heat
Little feet come out of shoes
Busy people start to snooze
And in the fields all over the world
In the fields all over the world
Grasses grow, winds blow
And the bees in the apple trees
Buzz, Buzz, Buzz
Dream in the solemn heat.

Sleep like a Rabbit

Sleep like a rabbit, sleep like a bear.
Sleep like the old cat under the chair.
Sleep like a rabbit, sleep like a bear.
Sleep like the old cat under the chair.

Tuck in your paws and lower your head.
Close your blinking eyes so red.
Take a deep breath on your rabbit bed
And now lie down.

Sleep like a polar bear asleep in the sea,
Flat on his back afloat in the sea,
Up on the waves like a boat in the sea,
Snoozing away like a bear on the sea.

Sleep like a rabbit, sleep like a bear.
Sleep like the old cat under the chair.
Sleep like a rabbit, sleep like a bear.
Sleep like the old cat under the chair.

Why so sleepy little mole,
Curled and tightly sleeping?
There is no noise beneath the ground
And no worms sing.

Little squirrel up in a tree,
Resting there so sleepily,
Fluffy tail about your head
In your little wind-rocked bed.
Curl up there so sleepy.

Sleep like a rabbit, sleep like a bear.
Sleep like the old cat under the chair.
Sleep like a rabbit, sleep like a bear.
Sleep like the old cat under the chair.

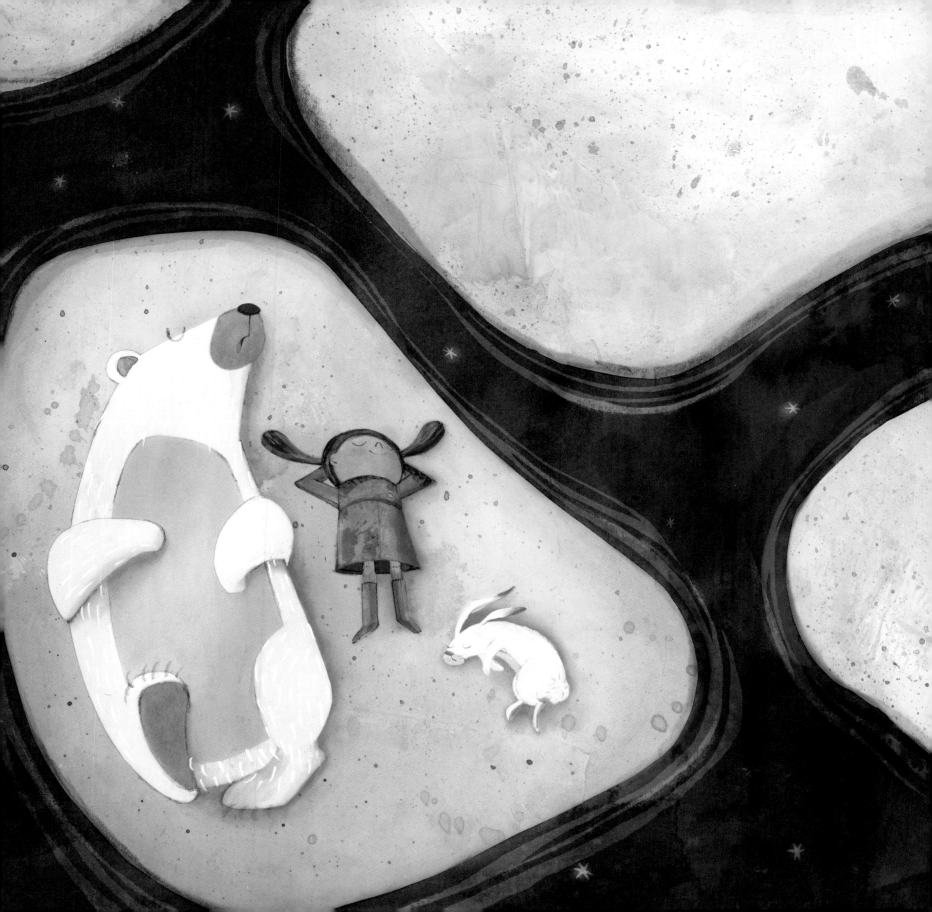

bunny jig

Big and little,

Little and big.
A little bunny
And a big fat pig.
Big or little,
Little or big.
Stomp your feet
And dance a jig.

Little or big
Dance a jig
With a bug
Or a bunny
And an old fat pig.
Big or little,
Little or big.
Stomp your feet
And dance a jig.

WHEN THE MAN IN THE MOON WAS A LITTLE BOY

When the man in the moon was a little boy,
Sing hi ho, the man in the moon,
He ran away with a shooting star.
Ho hum, the man in the moon.

And pretty soon in the dark of the moon
And the sky was lit with an amber light
And all the stars began to fight
By blinking at each other.

When the man in the moon was a little boy,
Sing hi ho, the man in the moon,
He ran away with a shooting star.
Ho hum, the man in the moon.

And they winked
And they blinked
In the enormous night
Till the sun came up
And drove them out of sight
And all the stars began to fight
By blinking at each other.

When the man in the moon was a little boy,
Sing hi ho, the man in the moon.

Advice to Bunnies

Bunny, Sleepy Bunny,
Sleepy Bun Bun,
Don't go to sleep
In the day's hot sun.
Keep one eye open
And twitch your nose.
Keep your nose twitching
When the wind blows.

Bunny, Sleepy Bunny,
Sleepy Bun Bun,
Thump on the ground
When it's time to run.
Keep one ear up
And one ear down.
Never go near
A house or a town.

Bunny, Sleepy Bunny,
Sleepy Bun Bun,
When the moon is full
You can have your fun!

Song to Estyn

Baby, sail the seven seas
Safely in my arms.
When the waves go up and down,
You are safe from harm.

While the breezes gently blow,
You rock to and fro.
When the gale blows from the south,
You will sail and go.

Baby, sail the seven seas
Safely in my arms.
When the waves go up and down,
You are safe from harm.

When the ocean's white with spray,
You will sail away
Until the rising sun
Ends the voyage just begun.

Baby, sail the seven seas
Safely in my arms.
When the waves go up and down,
You are safe from harm.

While the breezes gently blow,
You rock to and fro.
When the gale blows from the south,
You will sail and go.

Baby, sail the seven seas
Safely in my arms.
When the waves go up and down,
You are safe from harm.

When the ocean's white with spray,
You will sail away
Until the rising sun
Ends the voyage just begun.

Fall of the Year

The world's on fire in the cold clear air
The world shouts AUTUMN everywhere.
All the little animals began to grow more fur,
All the summer birds began to fly away,
The little gray kitten came out of the wind to purr,
And the leaves blew away. All in one day.

Darkness came before the night
The air grew cold enough to bite
Chrysanthemums were shaggy yellow
The leaves turned red
The leaves turned brown
They tumbled all over the frosty ground
The world's on fire in the cold clear air
The world shouts AUTUMN everywhere.

THE SECRET SONG

Who saw the petals
Drop from the rose?
"I," said the spider.
"But nobody knows."

Who saw the sunset
Flash on a bird?
"I," said the fish.
"But nobody heard."

Who saw the fog
Come over the sea?
"I," said the sea pigeon.
"Only me."

Who saw the first green light
Of the sun?
"I," said the night owl.
"The only one."

Who saw the moss
Creep over the stone?
"I," said the gray fox.
"All alone."

Who saw the fog
Come over the sea?
"I," said the sea pigeon.
"Only me."

QUIET IN THE WILDERNESS

A hedgehog lived in the wilderness
Far from the noises of machines and men
Quiet of the sky
And the sun
And the moon
And the sea
And then
A crow cawed
The wind reared
A bird chirped
A bird sang
A bee buzzed
And the heavy wings of a gull
Beat slowly on the air

And everywhere
In the silence all around
The wind stirred
Grass and branch
And came roaring down the woods
And roared away.
A coot beat the waters of the sea
In the silence all around
In the silence of the sea
In the silence of nowhere
In the silence of the sea
A fish jumped
The seaweed popped and the sand sighed
In the low tide.

WOODEN TOWN

In the wooden town,
In the wooden town,
The streets ran up
And the streets ran down.
And there wasn't a sound,
There was no one around,
In the late night hour
In the wooden town.

In the wooden town,
In the wooden town,
The streets ran up
And the streets ran down.
And there wasn't a sound,
There was no one around,
In the late night hour
In the wooden town.

In the wooden town,
The streets ran up
And the streets ran down.
And there wasn't a sound
In the late night hour
In the wooden town.

In the wooden town,
There wasn't a sound.
In the wooden town,
There wasn't a sound.

In the wooden town,
The streets ran up
And the streets ran down.
And there wasn't a sound
In the late night hour
In the wooden town,
In the wooden town,
In the wooden town,
In the wooden town.

THE Kitten's Dream

He heard a bird
He heard a flea
He thought he heard a linden tree
Singing to a bumblebee.
He heard the rain
He heard a train
He thought he heard the Queen of Spain
Gayly whistling an old refrain.
He heard a fish jump in the lake
He had a fight with a birthday cake
He heard himself begin to sing
And dreamed he was awake.

LITTLE DONKEY CLOSE YOUR EYES

Little Donkey on the hill,
Standing there so very still,
Making faces at the skies.
Little Donkey, close your eyes.

Little Monkey in the tree,
Swinging there so merrily,
Throwing coconuts at the skies.
Little Monkey, close your eyes.

Silly Sheep that slowly crop,
Night has come and you must stop
Chewing grass beneath the skies.
Silly Sheep, now, close your eyes.
Little Pig that squeals about,

Make no noises with your snout.
No more squealing to the skies.
Little Pig, now, close your eyes.

Wild young birds that sweetly sing,
Curve your heads beneath your wing.
Dark night covers all the skies.
Wild young birds, now, close your eyes.

Old black cat down in the barn
Keeping five small kittens warm,
Let the wind blow in the skies.
Dear old black cat, close your eyes.

Little child all tucked in bed
Looking such a sleepy head,
Stars are quiet in the skies.
Little child, now, close your eyes.

Cherry Tree

There was a time
When the cherries were red
That I lay on the grass
And they fell on my head.

The birds chirped and sang
In the tree overhead
And I laughed in the grass
When the cherries were red.

But now my dear tree
Where the cherries were red
Is frozen and gray,
The birds are all fled.

I lie on the ground,
Snow falls on my head,
And I dream of the time
When the cherries were red.

When I Close My Eyes at Night

When I close my eyes at night,
In the darkness I see light,
Blue clouds in a big white sky.

When I close my eyes at night,
In the darkness I see light,
Where bright green birds go flying by.

When I close my eyes at night,
In the darkness I see light,
Blue clouds in a big white sky.

When I close my eyes at night,
In the darkness I see light,
Bright green birds go flying by.

Winter Adventure

Once I followed rabbit tracks
    Up to a hollow tree.
When I looked in
    A rabbit looked out at me.

His ears were down,
    His eyes were bright,
And his nose twitched
    Constantly.

I put an apple there
    For his delight
Then I stepped back—
    One step,
        Two steps,
            Three—
He shot like a bullet
    From out of that tree
Leaving tracks in the snow,
    And the apple there for me.

Sounds in the Night

They come softly at first
As cars go by,
As boats whistle
Far away, as dogs bark,
Far away in the night.
The boats and the whistles
And the wheels on the street
And the things people said
All day.
All far, far away.
And night
And sleep.

Snowfall

In the soft mysterious fall of the snow
The bell buoys ring
The whistles blow
While boats go slowly through the snow
Over the river, to and fro.

Slow, Slow
In the soft mysterious fall of the snow
Walking in wonder
The children go
Home from school, their laughter low
Catching falling flakes of snow.

Slow, Slow
In the soft mysterious fall of the snow
Light in the air
And deep below
Through the trees all white with snow
The lights of evening softly glow.

The Mouse's Prayer

Close my eyes and go to sleep.
Bugs no more on grass blades creep.
Bugs no more and birds no more,
In the woods will come no more

Dream of a weed growing from a seed,
Quietly, quietly from a seed.
In a garden
A slim green weed,
Quietly, quietly from a seed.

Close my eyes and go to sleep.
Bugs no more on grass blades creep.
Bugs no more and birds no more,
In the woods will come no more.

Dream of a mouse
In a quiet house
Saying his prayers
On the back stairs.
Please, please, please,
He prays for a piece of cheese.

Close my eyes and go to sleep.
Bugs no more on grass blades creep.
Bugs no more and birds no more,
In the woods will come no more.

Close my eyes and go to sleep.
Bugs no more on grass blades creep.
Bugs no more and birds no more,
In the woods will come no more.

JONATHAN BEAN earned an MFA from the School of Visual Arts and then dove right into the world of picture book illustration. His first two picture books, *At Night* and *Building Our House*, each won a Boston Globe-Horn Book Award. He is also the illustrator of two acclaimed picture books by Lauren Thompson, *The Apple Pie That Papa Baked,* which won the Ezra Jack Keats Award, and *One Starry Night*. Jonathan lives and works in Harrisburg, Pennsylvania.

"The art for "The Mouse's Prayer" was made with black and white ink drawings, one for each color. The drawings were then scanned digitally, overlaid, and assigned colors in Photoshop.

CARIN BERGER is the award-winning creator of several picture books, including *Forever Friends, Ok Go!,* and *The Little Yellow Leaf,* named one of the *New York Times* Ten Best Illustrated Books of 2008. Carin and her family divide their time between New York City and the Berkshires.

"I grew up with the 'great green room' from *Goodnight Moon*. It was almost a tangible space in my mind, and so when I began to illustrate 'When I Close My Eyes at Night' I could almost picture the narrator peering out of the window of that room. I built the illustration as a little 3D stage and photographed it with Porter Gillespie to create a dreamy, not-quite-real atmosphere."

SOPHIE BLACKALL has illustrated more than thirty books for children including the *New York Times* bestselling series Ivy and Bean and the Caldecott Medal-winning *Finding Winnie*. Originally from Australia, Sophie now makes her home in Brooklyn, New York. She has traveled to India with UNICEF and returned with a head full of peacocks, chattering children, moonlit temples, and patterned saris, all of which inspired her painting for "Mambian Melody."

LEO ESPINOSA is an illustrator from Bogotá, Colombia, whose work has been featured in animated series, gallery shows, and publications, including *The New Yorker, Wired, Esquire,* and the *New York Times*. Leo's illustrations have been recognized by *American Illustration, 3x3,* and *Communication Arts*, and have been awarded Gold and Silver Medals from The Society of Illustrators. He lives with his family in Salt Lake City, Utah.

"To illustrate 'Fall of the Year,' my work began while walking my dog. I listened to the crunch of leaves under our feet and watched the afternoon light, which reminded me of the extraordinary autumns in New England. Later in the studio I created the composition with paper and pencil before rendering all the material on the computer."

BLANCA GÓMEZ is an illustrator living and working in Madrid, Spain. She started creating illustrations for her mother when she was a child. Now she illustrates for clients around the world, taking on projects ranging from interior design, to stationery, to advertising. Lately, she's been illustrating children's books, including *Besos for Baby: A Little Book of Kisses* and *One Family*.

"To illustrate 'The Song of the Tiny Cat' I wanted to re-create the atmosphere of the first nights of spring, when you can still feel the last winter chill, but the light is starting to feel more clear. I created the image by assembling textures and creating handmade collages on the computer."

MOLLY IDLE worked for DreamWorks Feature Animation Studios until she leapt into the world of children's book illustration. She is the creator of a plethora of whimsical picture books, including *Tea Rex, Camp Rex, Flora and the Penguin,* and *Flora and the Flamingo,* a 2014 Caldecott Honor book. Molly lives with her fabulous family in Tempe, Arizona.

"The bunnies in *Goodnight Moon* are iconic picture book creations. So it was such a treat to have the chance to illustrate my own moonlit, cotton-tailed characters inspired by Margaret Wise Brown, in 'Advice for Bunnies.'"

LINDA BLECK is the illustrator of numerous books for young readers, including Margaret Wise Brown's *The Moon Shines Down*; Deb Pilutti's *The City Kid and the Suburb Kid*, winner of Chicago Public Library's Best of the Best Award; and her own *Pepper Goes to School*, winner of a National Parenting Publication Award.

Linda has always been fascinated by the energy and excitement experienced on a full moon's night, when some creatures fall asleep and others are wide awake. Her illustration for "Goat on the Mountain" was inspired by her fond memories of growing up on an orchard. Plus, she has always wanted to draw a hedgehog.

PETER BROWN was working on animated TV shows when he signed a book deal to write and illustrate his first picture book, *Flight of the Dodo*. Since then he has written and illustrated more than a dozen books for children, including *The Curious Garden, Children Make Terrible Pets,* and *Mr. Tiger Goes Wild*. His books have earned numerous honors, including a Caldecott Honor, a Horn Book Award, two E. B. White Awards, a Children's Choice Award for Illustrator of the Year, and a *New York Times* Best Illustrated Book Award. Peter lives in Brooklyn, New York.

Peter created the illustration for "Love Song of the Little Bear" with India ink, watercolor, gouache, and pencil on paper, which he then digitally composited and colored.

FLOYD COOPER has illustrated more than 90 children's books, including *The Blacker the Berry, Brown Honey in Broomwheat Tea, and A Dance Like Starlight. Among the many awards his books have won are a Coretta Scott King Award,* three Coretta Scott King Honor Awards, the NAACP Image Award, and the Jane Addams Peace Honor. Floyd lives in Easton, Pennsylvania, with his wife and two sons.

The technique Floyd used to create the illustration for "To a Child" is called oil wash on board. He painted an illustration board with oil paint, and then erased the paint bit by bit with a stretchy eraser to make the picture. He likes to demonstrate this "subtractive process" for kids to show them "that there can be different approaches to age-old problems."

RENATA LIWSKA'S illustrations are influenced by memories of her childhood. She is the illustrator of the *New York Times* bestsellers *The Quiet Book* and *The Loud Book* by Deborah Underwood, and is the author and illustrator of *Little Panda* and *The Red Wagon*. Originally from Warsaw, Poland, Renata now lives in Calgary, Canada, with her husband, Mike.

"While visiting New York City, I was sketching in a lovely little cafe in Greenpoint, Brooklyn, when I received an email asking if I would consider creating the illustration for 'The Noon Balloon.' It caught my imagination right away and I had pretty much finished the drawing by the time I left the cafe. I learned later that the author of the poem, Margaret Wise Brown, was born in Greenpoint. It surely was meant to be!"

ELLY MACKAY'S work has been featured in *O Magazine, Cosmopolitan China, Flow,* and in the Original Art show at the Society of Illustrators. Her books include *If You Hold a Seed, Fall Leaves,* and *Butterfly Park*. She lives in Ontario, Canada, with her husband and their two children.

"I have been making little paper worlds since I was a child. I use ink to make small drawings that I cut out and set up in a miniature theatre. Then I light the scene and photograph it. I had fun experimenting with salt, translucent paper, yupo paper, ink, and spray paint to create the art for 'The Cherry Tree.' When I read this poem, I was transported back to some of my favourite days . . . snow days! I loved going out to explore, make snow angels, and feed the hearty chickadees."

CHRISTOPHER SILAS NEAL'S first picture book, *Over and Under the Snow* by Kate Messner, was praised in the *New York Times* for its "stunning retro-style illustrations," was a 2011 *New York Times* Editor's Choice, and won an E. B. White Honor Award in 2012. Christopher has directed short animated videos for Kate Spade and Anthropologie and was awarded a medal from the Society of Illustrators for his work in motion graphics. He lives in Brooklyn, New York, and teaches Illustration at Pratt Institute.

"What began as a sketched row of empty houses evolved organically into the finished art for 'Wooden Town,' with the houses stacked up as a road winds through them like a piece of red ribbon. Perhaps after years of being empty, these houses have begun to take on a life of their own."

ZACHARIAH OHORA has illustrated many picture books, include the *New York Times* bestselling *Wolfie the Bunny* by Ame Dyckman and *Stop Snoring Bernard!*, which won the 2011 Founder's Award at the Society of Illustrators and was the PA One Book for 2012. Zachariah lives and works in Narberth, Pennsylvania, with his wife, Lydia, sons Oskar and Theodore, and a fat cat named Teddy.

"I created the illustration for 'Little Donkey Close Your Eyes' in pen and ink, then added colors and textures digitally. I wanted to explore a limited nighttime palette while creating a realistic space where all these animals might co-exist."

ERIC PUYBARET studied illustration at the École Nationale Supérieure des Arts Décoratifs in Paris. Eric is the bestselling illustrator of *Puff, the Magic Dragon* by Peter Yarrow and Lenny Lipton, and *The Night Before Christmas* performed by Peter, Paul and Mary, along with numerous other books published in the United States and in his native France.

Eric created the artwork for "Song of Estyn" using acrylic paint on linen.

SEAN QUALLS has illustrated many books for children, including *Giant Steps to Change the World* by Spike Lee and Tonya Lewis-Lee and *Before John Was a Jazz Giant* by Carole Boston Weatherford, for which Sean received a Coretta Scott King Illustration Honor. Sean draws inspiration from many influences including Black memorabilia, Americana, outsider art, cave paintings, mythology, music, and vintage children's books. He lives in Brooklyn, New York, with his wife, illustrator/author Selina Alko, and their two children.

While creating the illustration for "When the Man in the Moon Was a Little Boy," Sean listened to a special playlist of moon-themed songs.

ISABEL ROXAS is an illustrator and graphic designer born and raised in the Philippines. Currently, she creates picture books, builds tiny sculptures, and designs paper goods in her Brooklyn studio. A whimsical artist, she has a taste for the slightly odd and uncommon, and for tales that go awry. She illustrated *The Case of the Missing Donut* written by Alison McGhee and *Day at the Market* by May Tobias-Papa, which won the Philippine Children's National Book Award in 2010.

"'Sleep like a Rabbit' is such a quiet, drowsy poem that when I was dreaming up ideas for the illustration, I tried to think of the quietest place one could sleep—which brought to mind snow and how it muffles street noises, and also the stillness of ice. I worked with found paper and paint, and enhanced the final piece on the computer."

DADU SHIN has always loved picture books and is delighted to now be working on picture book projects of his own. He also does illustration work in the editorial and fashion markets, and has been awarded two Silver Medals from The Society of Illustrators. Dadu lives and works in Brooklyn, New York.

Many of Dadu's illustrations are inspired by nature, perhaps because he grew up around the woods of Massachusetts. He has fond memories of being in the wilderness surrounded by trees and animals. Many of these memories inspired the art created for "Quiet in the Wilderness." He remembers in particular the subtle stillness of the woods, which he tried to capture in his illustration for the poem.

DAVID SMALL has written and/or illustrated over 50 picture books, including *Imogene's Antlers*. His many awards and honors include the Caldecott Medal and two Caldecott Honors. His graphic memoir *Stitches* was a National Book Award Finalist. He and his wife, the writer Sarah Stewart, live in a historic home on the bend of a river in southwest rural Michigan. Living in the country for many years, David has been personally acquainted with many bunnies, pigs, and bugs.

"In 'Bunny Jig,' Margaret Wise Brown seems to be poking gentle fun at those who make curious choices of partners in the dance of life. I chose to expand the tale, to make it into a short-short story, following Mr. Bunny as he frolics with two odd consorts, leaving much to the viewer's imagination, including: 'What were they all *thinking*?!!'"

BOB STAAKE is the author and/or illustrator of over 60 books including *The Donut Chef*; *Bluebird,* a *New York Times* Notable Book; and *The Red Lemon*, a *New York Times* Best Illustrated Children's Book. He is also the creator of many of *The New Yorker*'s most iconic covers of recent years, including the magazine's all-time bestseller, "Reflection," which commemorated Barack Obama's historic 2008 presidential win. Bob lives and works in a 200-year-old house on the elbow of Cape Cod, Massachusetts.

"I grew up reading Margaret Wise Brown's work, so of course I was honored to be asked to illustrate 'The Kitten's Dream.' It's such an evocative poem and her text alone suggests some inspiring mental images. I just hope my colors, textures, and characters do justice to her beautiful words."

MELISSA SWEET is the author and illustrator of *Balloons Over Broadway*, which won the Robert F. Sibert Award for the most distinguished informational book for children. Among the nearly 100 other books she has illustrated are *A River of Words* by Jen Bryant, winner of a Caldecott Honor, and her own *Some Writer!* She lives in Rockport, Maine.

"The art for 'The Secret Song' was rendered in watercolor, gouache, collage, and pencil on Twinrocker paper. As I was started the piece, I took a ferry to a nearby island where Margaret Wise Brown once had a home. She referred to this house in Maine as 'The Only House,' and though I was not sure which white cottage dotting the coast was hers, it seemed fitting that the art for this poem reflect the wildness of the island."

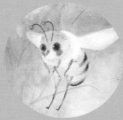

SATOE TONE is a children's book creator from Japan who currently lives in Italy. She has published a number of picture books that have been translated into Japanese, Italian, French, German, English, Korean, Chinese, and Spanish. Satoe was the 2013 winner of the International Award for Illustration at the Bologna Book Fair.

"I read 'Buzz, Buzz, Buzz' over and over, then closed my eyes, trying to imagine the field full of buzzing bees. Little by little, I created the scene in my mind: a hot, sleepy summer daydream. Sunlight poured through young apple trees. Bright summer flowers trembled in the breeze. I then tried to draw the scene as if it were a flashback. I repainted again and again, vivid colors on white. When I was painting it, I was in the world of 'Buzz, Buzz, Buzz.'"

FRANK VIVA is a frequent cover artist for *The New Yorker*. His first book, *Along a Long Road*, was a *New York Times* Best Illustrated Children's Book. His fourth book, *Young Frank, Architect*, was the first picture book ever created for The Museum of Modern Art's publications department, and has been translated into seven languages. Frank lives in Toronto, Canada.

"'Snowfall' has a gentle, surreal quality. The landscape described seems like something remembered from a dream. I wanted the art to have a similar quality. The children and boats are pushing through knee-high snow, and even the houses and trees appear to be doing the same thing. When looked at one way, everything is trudging in the same direction. Or the 'trail' might simply be windswept snow left on the leeward side of the stationary objects."

MICK WIGGINS has worked as a freelance illustrator for 30 years, mostly in the editorial and book publishing fields. He's received many awards, appeared in numerous juried art annuals, and has enjoyed a long and varied list of clients. Mick's work includes several picture books, covers for the works of John Steinbeck for Penguin Classics, and several postage stamps for the USPS. Mick currently lives Little Rock, Arkansas.

"I've always enjoyed discovering all the small details found in picture book illustrations and really hope to inspire the same with my images. With 'Winter Adventure,' I saw the opportunity to use the final stanza as a way of almost telling the story in reverse—whereby the eye is lead back in time to the introduction of the story."

DAN YACCARINO is the author and illustrator of many children's books including *Doug Unplugged*, *Unlovable*, and *The Fantastic Undersea Life of Jacques Cousteau*. He is also the creator and producer of two animated series, the Parents Choice Award-winning *Oswald* and the Emmy Award–winning *Willa's Wild Life,* as well as the character designer behind the Emmy Award–winning *The Backyardigans*. His books have won a host of prestigious awards including the *New York Times* Best Illustrated award, an ALA Notable designation, and the Bologna Ragazzi. Dan lives with his family in New York City.

The illustration for "Sounds in the Night" was created with brush and ink on vellum, and Photoshop.

Follow these links for accompanying songs to wish a child goodnight (included as bonus CDs in the hardcover editions of *Goodnight Songs* and *A Celebration of the Seasons: Goodnight Songs*):

store.cdbaby.com/cd/tomprouttandemilygary

store.cdbaby.com/cd/tomprouttandemilygary2

TOM PROUTT and EMILY GARY, singer/songwriters known as the duo "Tom and Emily," have beautifully and respectfully translated the poetry of Margaret Wise Brown to music in a way that will captivate listeners of all ages. Using the language of voice and instrumentation, they've created a soundscape that's joyful and gentle, fanciful and fun. For more information about their music, visit them online at tomandemilymusic.com.